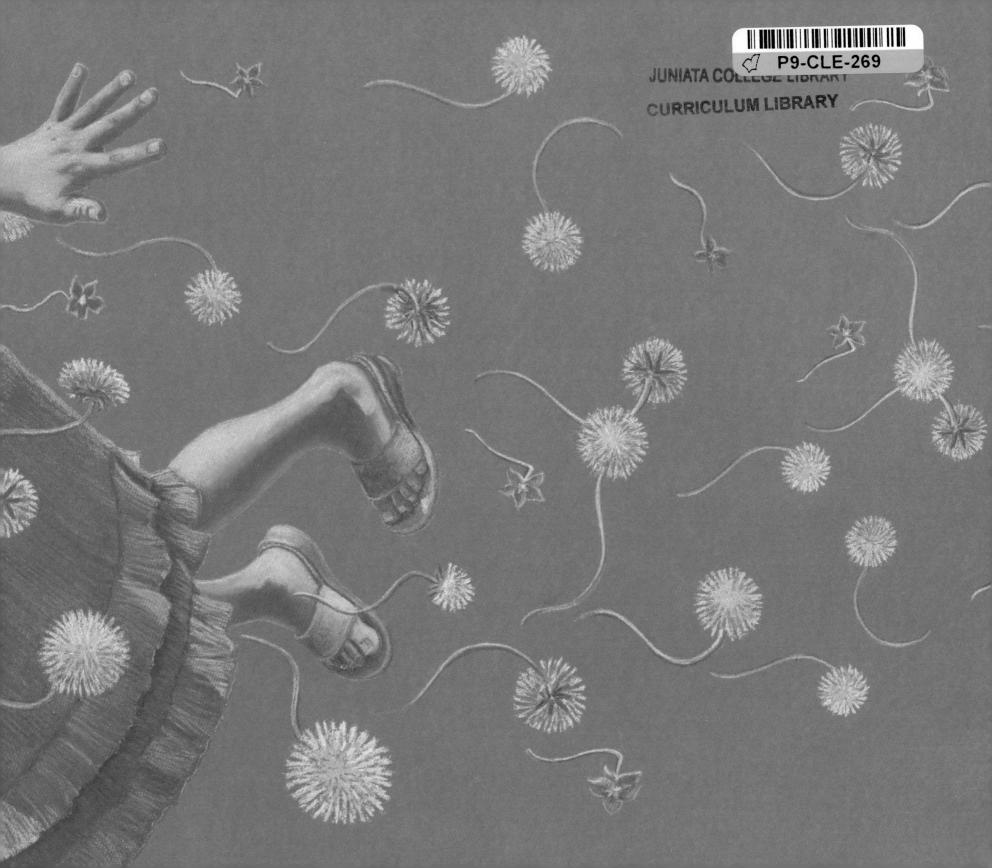

A Walk With Grandpa

Written by Sharon K. Solomon

Illustrated by Pamela Barcita

A Walk With Grandpa

To my wonderful husband Howard – Sharon
For José and Miranda – Pamela

To the woodlands, riverscapes and creatures of
Northwest River Park in Chesapeake, Virginia,
the inspiration for this visual journey.

Text ©2009 by Sharon K. Solomon
Illustration ©2009 by Pamela Barcita

Solomon, Sharon K.

A Walk With Grandpa / written by Sharon K. Solomon; illustrated by Pamela Barcita;
1st ed. – McHenry, IL, Raven Tree Press. 2009.

p. ; cm.

SUMMARY: Daniela and her grandpa take a walk in the woods
and share what they mean to each other.

English Edition
ISBN: 978-1-934960-11-0   Hardcover
ISBN: 978-1-934960-12-7   Paperback

Audience: pre-K to 3rd grade.

1. Family/Multigenerational – Juvenile fiction.
2. Concepts/Opposites – Juvenile fiction.
I. Illust. Barcita, Pamela.   II. Title.

Library of Congress Control Number: 2008932221

Printed in Taiwan
10 9 8 7 6 5 4 3 2 1

First Edition

Free activities for this book are available at www.raventreepress.com

Raven Tree Press
A Division of Delta Systems Co., Inc.
www.raventreepress.com

One sunny day,
Daniela and her grandpa went for a walk.
They played a silly word game
as they walked along.

"You are my sunshine,"
said Grandpa.

4

"You are my moonshine,"
giggled Daniela.

"You are my earth."

"You are my sky."
She squeezed his hand.

"You are my summer."

"You are my winter."

"You are my question."

"And you are my answer."

"You are my day."

"You are my night."

"You are my hello."

14

"You are my good—bye."

15

"You are my lost."

16

"And you are my found."

17

They sat on the big gray rock,
looking down at the river.
Daniela kicked her feet as she watched
their reflections in the water.

Then, she hugged her grandpa.
"I love you, Pop Pop," she said.
"And I love you, my little Tulip,"
said Grandpa.

Soon it was time to go home.
"You are my friend," said Daniela.

"You are my pal,"
Grandpa replied.

21

"You are my music."

"You are my song."

"You are my hope."

"You are my wish."

"You are my happy."

"You are my glad."

"You are my super grandpa," Daniela said.

"And you are
my wonderful granddaughter,"
Grandpa replied.

"Let's walk again tomorrow," said Daniela.
Grandpa nodded with a smile.

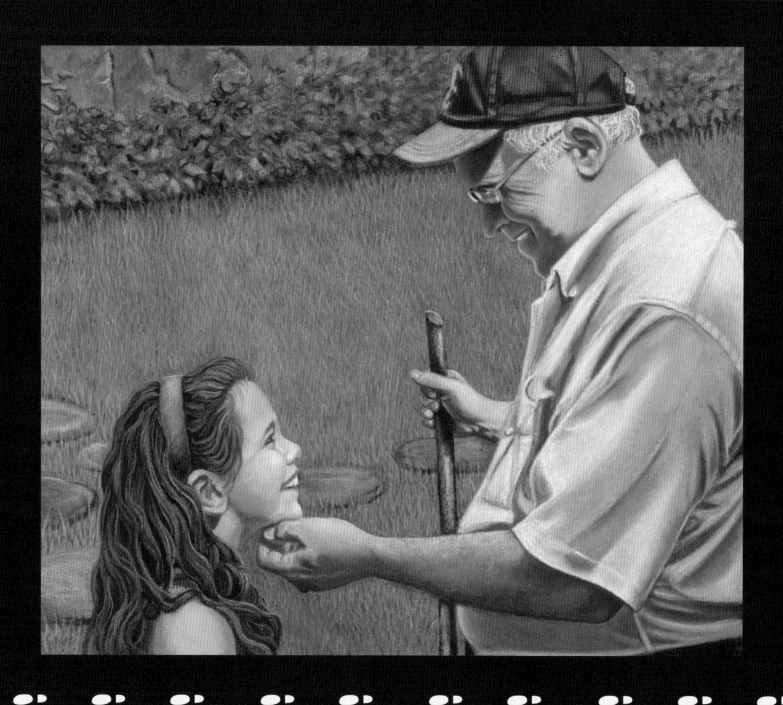